To Louis,

Victoria Blay

Tom's Bobble

Bumblebee Books
London

BUMBLEBEE PAPERBACK EDITION

A CIP catalogue record for this title is
available from the British Library.

ISBN: 978-1-83934-628-6

Bumblebee Books is an imprint of
Olympia Publishers.

First Published in 2022

Bumblebee Books
Tallis House
2 Tallis Street
London
EC4Y 0AB

Printed in Great Britain

www.olympiapublishers.com

Dedication

For Dylan and Mr Blithers.

There was once a cat called Tom. Tom lived in a dustbin by the fish market. Even though he slept in a dustbin, he liked to stay clean and always looked smart. He had fuzzy white paws, a thick orange coat, and bright green eyes.

Every morning Tom strolled over to the market to greet his fishmonger friends. The fishmongers liked Tom very much.

Mr Blithers was Tom's favourite fishmonger because he always fed him kippers. "What a well-mannered cat you are!" said Mr Blithers as he patted Tom on the head.

BLITHERS
KIPPERS
BLITHERS
KIPPERS

Tom was indeed a well-mannered, charming and handsome cat, but he had one problem. A rather big problem for a cat… Tom had no tail.

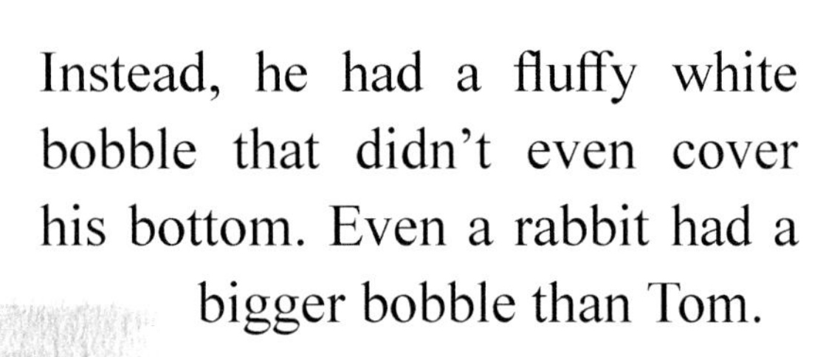

Instead, he had a fluffy white bobble that didn't even cover his bottom. Even a rabbit had a bigger bobble than Tom.

Tom checked his bobble every day to see if it had grown.

Sometimes he felt sad because he was the only cat who didn't have a tail.

Tom often thought of different ways to help his bobble grow. Once, he asked his best friend, Dodger, to water his bobble every day for a whole week.

No matter what they tried…

Tom’s bobble NEVER GREW!

It was Christmas Eve. Tom imagined waking up on Christmas Day to discover his bobble had sprouted into a long and magnificent tail.

Suddenly Tom's thoughts were interrupted. "Merry Christmas, Tom, I made you a gift!" Tom opened one eye, it was Dodger.
"But it's not Christmas Day yet!" said Tom. Dodger was far too excited to wait until Christmas day.

Tom sat up and opened his gift. “It’s a sock tail,” blurted Dodger, “do you like it?”
“I love it!” said Tom with a big smile.

Every Christmas, Dodger made Tom a gift. Last Christmas, he made him a hat out of an old tea cosy.

The Christmas before that, he collected shells from the market floor and made Tom a necklace.

Tom fastened the ribbons around his bobble and tested out his new tail. How marvellous it looked!

Tom and Dodger hadn't noticed the clowder of cats staring at Tom's new tail. One cat crept forward and gave it a sharp tug! Tom fell over and all the cats began to laugh.
"You'll never be like us," said one cat.
"You'll always be the 'Tailless Tom'," shouted another.

Dodger hissed and swiped the sock tail back, and stuffed it into his satchel.

He hurried after Tom who was racing towards Mr Blither's stall.

Mr Blithers was busy talking to a customer when the two cats bolted under the fish counter. Distracted by the commotion, the lady customer bent down and lifted the tablecloth. “That poor cat hasn’t got a tail!” she said.

"That's Tom," chuckled Mr Blithers. "He is a Manx cat and comes from the Isle of Man where many of the cats don't have tails. My aunt lives there and as soon as I've sold these last few kippers, I'll catch the evening ferry to pay her a Christmas visit."

"Well then," said the lady customer, "I'll buy them all, so you can be on your way!" Mr Blithers wrapped the kippers and placed them in her basket. "Merry Christmas!" said the lady customer.

"And a Merry Christmas to you too," said Mr Blithers.

“So, you’re a ‘Manx cat’!” announced Dodger, with great excitement. “Come on, there’s no time to lose.” He sprung to his feet and ran across the road to Mr Blither’s motorcycle.

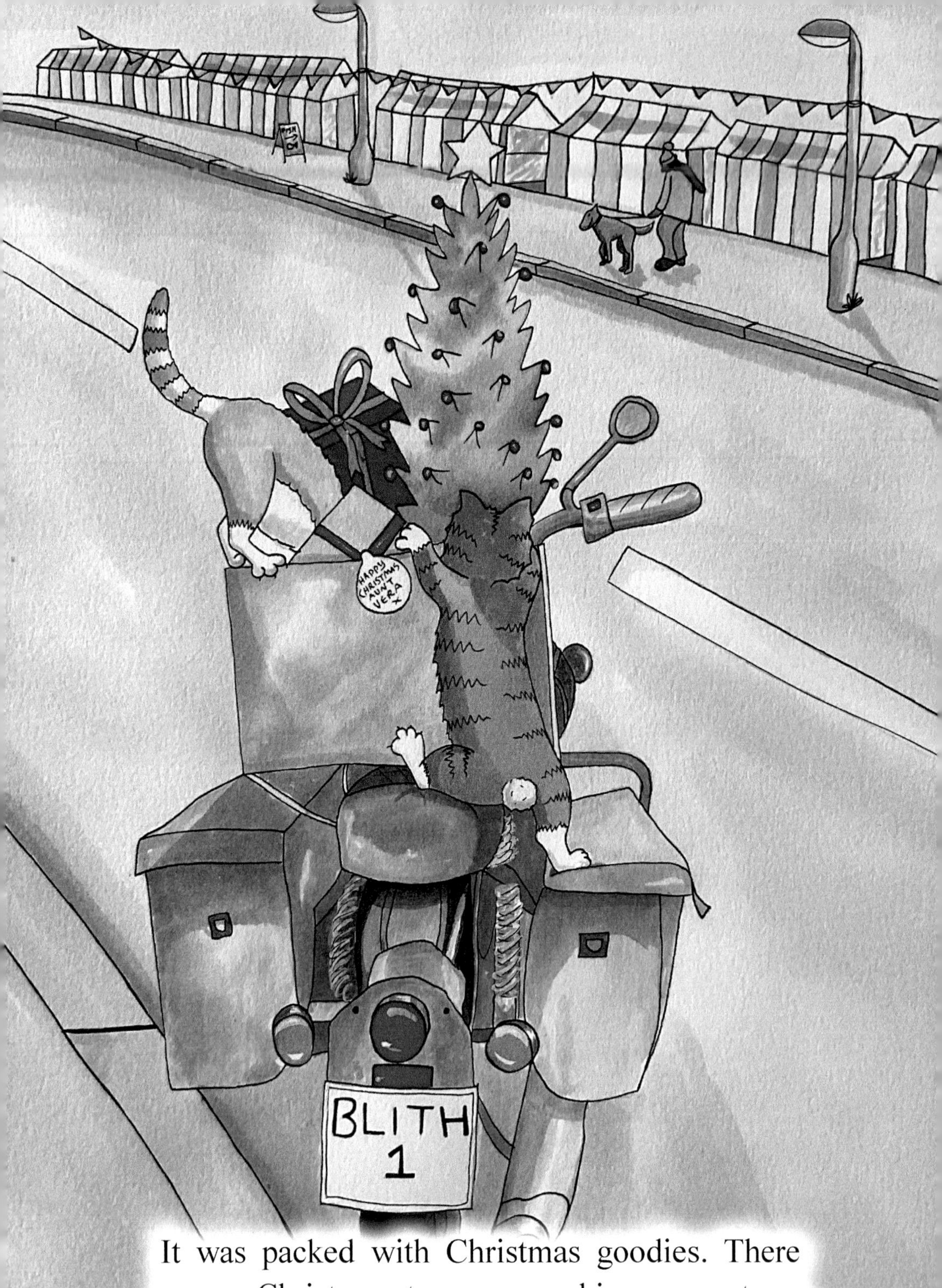

It was packed with Christmas goodies. There was a Christmas tree, some shiny presents, a large figgy pudding, and just enough space for Tom and Dodger to squeeze in and hide.

The cats waited patiently for Mr Blithers to arrive. He put on his helmet and gloves

and started up the engine.

Vroom! They were off!

BLITH
1

Mr Blithers rode all the way to the ferry. The cats nestled down and soon fell fast asleep.

They sailed all night

until it was light.

Dodger woke up and looked around.
“We’re on a ferry!” he said with great excitement.
“And it’s Christmas Day!” yawned Tom.

Suddenly, there was a loud ‘clunk’. The ferry door opened and Dodger jumped back into the box. Mr Blithers returned from his cabin and got back on his motorcycle. Vroom! They were off again.

The trees whizzed by

and the snow began to fall

and they all rode on.

Finally, they arrived at a little yellow cottage.

Aunt Vera appeared in the doorway holding her cat, Geoffrey.

Mr Blithers parked his motorcycle and went over to greet them.

"Look, Tom! That cats got a bobble just like you!" said Dodger.
Tom lent out of the box for a better look.
He lent a bit too far…

The box slipped and the cats tumbled onto the floor with a...

CRASH!

"It's Tom and Dodger!" said Mr Blithers. "The homeless cats from the fish market!"
"Oh my!" said Aunt Vera. "They must be hungry after such a long journey."

Mr Blithers followed Aunt Vera into the cottage to fetch the cats some milk and kippers.

Geoffrey sat looking at Tom, and Tom sat looking at Geoffrey.

“You have a bobble like me,” said Tom.

“Yes, and I’m very proud of it!” said Geoffrey.

Just then another cat strolled over. Soon, Aunt Vera's Garden was bustling with cats of many kinds. There were cats with long tails, cats with short tails, cats with half tails, and cats with no tails! "I'm called a 'rumpy'," said one cat. "I don't have a tail, just a tuft of fur sticking out."

"Well I've got a stumpy tail," said a second cat.

"And I've got a riser," said the third cat, who proudly turned around to show it off.

Dodger smiled and pulled the sock tail out of his satchel. “I don’t think you’ll need this anymore, Tom!” All the cats began to laugh and so did Tom and Dodger.

It was a wonderful Christmas day. The cats sang Christmas carols

and played 'Catch the Jingle bell'.

Tom especially liked the game 'Pin the bobble on the cat'.

Aunt Vera adopted Tom and Dodger and said it was the best Christmas, she had ever had.

Tom and Dodger were very happy too. They now had a place they could both call home.

Acknowledgements

Thank you to my husband, son, mum and dad.
You have all been so encouraging... and patient!